Hi, my name is Hayden.
I'm nine years old at the time
of writing this book. I live in
California. It's been a dream of
mine the past couple of years to
write and illustrate a book about
some of my current interests in

science, sea animals, amphibians, reptiles, endangered
animals, Minecraft, and more! I read many books on
these subjects, watch videos, play Minecraft in creative
mode, sketch, and draw in 3D and with the computer.

When I heard that Minecraft was going to add
an axolotl to the game, a special type of salamander,
I immediately started having a lot of ideas about
the adventures the axolotl could go on. These ideas
quickly turned into stories that I began putting onto
these pages. I hope you enjoy reading the axolotl's big
adventures!

I'd also like to say, "Thank you." Thank you to
my parents, Nana, Rhonda Asbenson and wonderful
teachers throughout the years who continue to guide
me in realizing my dreams and expressing my ideas
through writing and art.

The Axolotl: Nether Adventures In Minecraft
Written and Illustrated by Hayden Coles

This book follows the Mojang commercial usage guidelines:

- This book is not an official Minecraft product and is not approved by or associated with Mojang.
- Mojang has no liability for this product or purchase.
- This product's seller and manufacturer/publisher is not Mojang, not associated with, or supported by Mojang.
- All rights (including copyright, trademark rights, and related rights) in the Minecraft name, brand, assets, and any derivatives are and will remain owned by Mojang.

Published by Dougy Press
dougypress.com

ISBN: 978-0-9797132-6-2

Contents

CHAPTER 1

CREATING A PORTAL

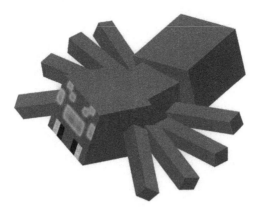

D oug has recently found a mineshaft that cats use to find gems. After the cats lead him to a portal, he's now thinking of ways to reconstruct the damaged portal. He's thinking of replacing the cracked obsidian with normal obsidian. He asks permission from the cats to remake the portal, and the cats say, "Yes" in quiet voices.

A few minutes later, while Doug is removing the cracked obsidian, he finds a special type of obsidian with glowing purple cracks through it and purple particles falling from it in liquid form. It looks like it's crying, and so Doug calls it "crying obsidian." It takes him a long time to mine it, but when he's done, the block glows twice as bright!

Doug wonders if the crying obsidian will be useful for anything but doesn't come up with any new ideas. Once he removes all the cracked obsidian, he asks the cats if they've found a lava chamber. The cats lead him down to the chamber at the lowest level. In the chamber, he sees a few diamonds on the ceiling that have formed because of the heat of the lava. He also notices a small water stream in a nearby unexplored cave.

Doug has recently read a book and learned that if he takes a bucket of water and pours it into the lava, there is a high chance the lava will turn into obsidian. He then travels through the darkness of the cave into the underground stream. He gets out his steel bucket and gets a scoop of water.

When he returns to the lava chamber, he hears a crawling sound on one of the nearby walls. A small, navy-blue spider jumps out of the darkness. What Doug doesn't know is that this isn't a normal spider. As the spider slowly moves closer, it bites him! Its bite is toxic, and he falls motionless on the ground!

CHAPTER 2

INTO FIRE

Doug doesn't know how to cure himself from the poisonous bite, but after much thinking, he realizes the cure: MILK!

He looks in his inventory and finds a milk bucket with a tiny bit of milk in it, but is it enough to cure him? Doug slurps down the milk. It doesn't taste good because it was left out too long, but it works!

Soon Doug is cured, and he removes the spider with his sword so that it can't poison him again! He eventually gains enough strength to hold the pail of water and brings it to the lava, gently pouring it into the lava. Most of the lava turns into cobblestone, but some turns into obsidian, perfect for building a portal. He finally gets back to the portal and removes the cracked obsidian and replaces it with the obsidian he's made.

Once Doug places the last piece of obsidian, nothing happens. Doug exclaims, "I expected the portal to open up and lots of lights would come out of it—not this!" He walks back to the cats and asks what happened.

Ankh says, "Oh, we just forgot. You need flint and steel to open the portal."

Doug asks, "How do I get flint and steel?"

Oreo answers, "First, you need a piece of flint, and then you need a piece of iron."

"Where do I find flint?" Doug asks.

Oreo replies, "You can rarely find it in gravel, but be advised, your flint and steel won't last forever."

Shortly after, Doug leaves the mine and starts his journey back to his base. On his way, he travels through an unexplored part of the mesa. There are giant terracotta spikes scattered throughout the sand, and he even must cross over a plateau. A few days later, he finally gets back to his base.

The next time he plans to go to the portal, he wants the axolotls, Geode and Blurple, to come with him. Doug then looks through his special chests and finds a few pieces of flint and a piece of iron. He walks to his crafting table and combines the two items. What's left is flint and steel.

Doug walks outside of his base and tries the flint and steel on a tree. He brushes the steel with the flint, and a slight spark appears. The spark goes onto the tree, and soon the tree is burning! Luckily the fire is contained because no other trees are nearby to cause a forest fire!

Doug walks back to his base and remembers that before he left the mesa, the cats told him an important message: the other dimension through the portal may be very hot and could possibly contain lava. Just in case, Doug tries different materials. His special netherite is the best and is fireproof. Doug makes plans to turn it into special buckets for Geode and Blurple.

Eventually, Doug crafts two almost perfectly made netherite buckets! He tests them by dropping the buckets in lava. The buckets float smoothly across the lava. Finally, Doug thinks that he and the axolotls will be ready to go into the other dimension.

After a few days, Doug and the axolotls arrive back at the mine and are about to light the portal. Doug brushes the flint against the steel. A small spark flies out and hits the bottom of the portal. Suddenly, the opening of the portal fills with an eerie purple glow and then a purple wall with many sparkles in it. He takes a step into the portal. He puts his foot through. Neither Doug nor the axolotls can see on the other side, but his foot feels tingly. Doug takes another step, and another, and another, and soon Doug's whole body is enveloped into the wall, and there is no trace of him or the axolotls!

CHAPTER 3

A BURNING WORLD

When Doug, together with the axolotls, goes through to the other side, the Nether, he instantly feels hotter than when he was in the Overworld. As the purple particles fade, he looks around. There are no signs of life except for a few mushrooms and some red and blue trees.

As he walks closer to one of the red trees, he hears a whining sound, almost like a cry. He turns around in horror to see that there is a huge ghast behind him! It's white and appears to be friendly. As he walks closer to it, suddenly its red eyes open, and it shoots a fireball at Doug! The fireball strikes at his feet, and he's propelled into a red tree, losing his grip on the two buckets holding the axolotls! Geode and Blurple fall out of the buckets and land in the nearby lava stream! As Doug gets off the burning ground, he realizes that he doesn't have the buckets in his hands. He looks around and then sees two empty netherite buckets floating on the lava.

"Oh, no!" Doug exclaims. He rushes over to the lava stream. Suddenly, he sees a red head come out of the lava and realizes that the axolotls are on top of the head! As the head keeps rising, he realizes that it's a special type of mob called a strider that saves the axolotls. The sides of its head are dangling with string, and it has a sad face rather than a happy face.

The strider waddles slowly out of the lava carrying the axolotls. The strider turns light purple and starts to shake once it leaves the lava because it's so cold. And this time, Doug looks at the strider's feet and notices that thin pieces of netherite are attached to its feet, thus making them fireproof. Doug hears another cry and looks at the ghast. He thinks for a second and then has a plan for how to stop it. He grabs his netherite sword and waits for the ghast to launch another fireball at him. Once the fireball comes close to him, he deflects it with his netherite sword. The fireball bounces back and hits the ghast. The ghast disintegrates, and all that is left is a tear and a small pile of gunpowder.

CHAPTER 4
TO THE FORTRESS

Doug then looks at a nearby lava lake, and in the distance, he notices a huge fortress. It seems to be dark red and has many support pillars. Some walkways above the support pillars seem to be broken and cracked. Doug has an idea about being able to ride on the strider to the fortress.

But first, Doug will have to feed the strider and name him. Doug names the strider "Grump-Grump" because he has a sad face.

Doug notices that the strider needs to be warm. He takes a few pieces of netherite out of his pack and a few strings off the sides of his head and sews them together to make a warm, fireproof sweater for him.

Doug puts the sweater on Grump-Grump, and he's no longer cold.

Then Doug puts a saddle on Grump-Grump and sits on him. Grump-Grump slowly waddles back to the lava, and Doug successfully collects both netherite buckets and puts the axolotls in them.

When Grump-Grump doesn't seem to move toward the fortress-like Doug wants him to, he gets off the saddle and wonders why. He decides that Grump-Grump is hungry and needs food. He picks up a few mushrooms to do a taste test. Grump-Grump doesn't like the normal mushrooms, but he likes the blue mushrooms—the warped mushrooms—the most.

Whenever there are warped mushrooms growing nearby, Grump-Grump waddles out of the lava and picks them to eat. Then, Doug has an idea: by putting a warped mushroom on a fishing rod in front of Grump-Grump, he could lure him to the fortress! Doug tries his idea with the grumpy strider, and he's successful!

A few minutes later, Doug docks onto the fortress with the axolotls and Grump-Grump. Doug looks on the wall and sees that there are engravings on it. The first engraving is the face of a black skeleton. The description explains that whenever it strikes you, it's unlike any type of poison that leaves you with half a heart; instead, the strike destroys anyone it hits!

CHAPTER 5
FINDING DEBRIS

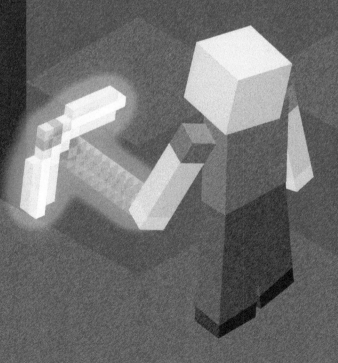

Doug is worried about encountering this type of skeleton. He walks past the engraving and moves on to the second one. It describes a box-like creature made of magma. If it gets destroyed, it'll create two smaller cubes that will keep attacking anyone in their path. These cubes also have a rock-like crust. As Doug walks to the next engraving, he hears something around the corner.

A floating head comes from the corner. Smoke forms below the head, and yellow rods circle around the smoke. Doug looks closely through the smoke and sees a small, fiery core in the center of the smoke. Doug names the creature "The Blaze."

Suddenly, The Blaze shoots an explosive fireball

at Doug. Grump-Grump seems to protect Doug from The Blaze. While Grump-Grump distracts The Blaze, Doug reaches through the black smoke and pulls out the core. The blazing rods suddenly fall to the ground. Doug picks up one of the rods; it's still hot. He collects the rest of the rods and puts them in his pack because they could be useful later.

Doug pets Grump-Grump and walks over to a wall. He grabs out his netherite pickaxe and starts mining the netherrack. Suddenly, he hits something. He looks at it for a second and then says, "I found Ancient Debris!"

CHAPTER 6

MAKING A MINE

Doug starts to mine the ancient debris. Once it's been collected, he thinks that the debris will drop a piece of netherite, but instead, it drops a netherite scrap. He's very disappointed that the debris did not drop netherite like he hoped. He keeps mining and figures that he might run into some gravel that will destroy him. He might even mine into a lava chamber.

Doug then walks over to the warped forest and collects a few pieces of warped wood. Suddenly, he hears a whining sound. He looks behind him to see that there is an angry ghast about to shoot a fireball at him! Doug dodges the fireball and grabs a fishing rod from his pack, throwing the hook at the ghast. Once the hook is set, Doug starts to reel him in. The ghast shoots another fireball, and Doug is quickly propelled into another tree. He sees a green figure come from behind the fortress. It's a creeper!

"This must be Cyan!" Doug exclaims.

Cyan has a netherite helmet and looks very excited. He runs to the ghast as fast as he can, and it explodes! The ghast disintegrates and drops a pile of gunpowder. Doug gets off the ground and asks if he's Cyan.

"Yes!" Cyan says happily.

Doug asks, "Can we be friends?"

Cyan replies, "OK!"

Doug tells Cyan his plan for building the mine, and Cyan asks if he can help.

Doug says, "Yay!"

He points to where he wants the mine to be built, and Cyan runs there as fast as he can. Eventually, Cyan runs into a netherrack wall and explodes. Soon Cyan has made a whole tunnel, perfect for finding ancient debris!

CHAPTER 7

UNCOVERING A BASTION

O nce Cyan is done with the mine, he asks Doug if the walls are unstable and if they need support. Doug grabs the warped wood blocks that he recently tried to get but was interrupted by the ghast. Doug uses the warped wood to make supports.

Cyan then asks if he can show Doug his home. Sadly, it's across a lava lake.

But Doug has a plan!

He makes a leather strap around Grump-Grump. On each side of Grump-Grump, there are leather pouches that can hold the axolotls in their buckets. Cyan then has enough room to jump on. They start, and Doug lures Grump-Grump across the lava lake.

Once they get to the other shore of the lava lake, Doug holds the axolotls' buckets and jumps off Grump-Grump. Cyan also jumps off Grump-Grump and leads the strider into his house.

Cyan's house is pretty cool, but the most important part of the house is that Cyan has his own aquarium! In the aquarium, there is a cyan axolotl. Even though it's called a cyan axolotl, it's a powder-blue color with pink frills. Cyan calls the axolotl "Snowy."

Doug asks, "How did you get the water into your aquarium? I tried to make an aquarium in the Nether, but whenever I let water out of my bucket, it always evaporates."

Cyan tells Doug how to make water in the Nether instructing, "First, you need to have some glow lichen. Then fill your aquarium of any size with lava. Make sure not to put your axolotl into your aquarium yet, or he'll be burned to a crisp! Next, put the glow lichen on the lava. You'll see that there is one small pool of water surrounded by blocks of obsidian. By continuing to break all the blocks of obsidian that form when water hits the lava, you can successfully make an aquarium in the Nether."

"Wow! That's so cool," Doug exclaims.

Cyan replies, "I recently found an unexplored structure on the lava lake far away. Let's go!"

Cyan walks to his armory. He grabs out his best pieces of TNT: charged TNT, fire TNT, and extra explosive TNT. Cyan puts on his best netherite helmet equipped with Blast Protection III, Protection III, and his own special enchantment called Explosive III. Explosive III makes his TNT three times as strong. The helmet repels any bad mobs away from Cyan.

Cyan gets onto the strider with the axolotls. They head to the unexplored structure. Once they reach the structure, Doug is amazed at how big it is.

"Wow!" Doug said, "This structure is basically a giant cube made out of dark bricks."

As they enter the huge cube, Doug doesn't want the axolotls to get hurt, so he leaves them with the strider, Grump-Grump, to play. The cube is mysteriously devoid of life. Doug calls the cube a "bastion remnant" because it's mostly broken and used to be part of a huge bastion tower.

CHAPTER 8

BREWING A POTION

T he cube is mostly filled with lava. There are a few stone paths that break into the lava. Doug is worried about falling into the lava, so he comes up with a plan. He reaches into his travel bundle and pulls out an enchanted brewing book. It's made with fine leather, and the pages are crafted from beautiful papyrus. Doug opens it and reads a page about how to make a potion. Doug needs to make a fire resistance potion. First, the brewing book says that you need to have a brewing stand in order to even make a potion. Doug asks Cyan if he has any cobblestone.

"Yes," Cyan says. He gives Doug the pieces of cobblestone.

Next, Doug needs a blaze rod. Luckily, when he

destroyed The Blaze, it dropped a blaze rod. Doug puts the blaze rod on top of the cobblestone, and it turns into a brewing table. Doug flips to the next page to see how to make a potion once the brewing stand is completed. He reads that the main ingredient to make any potion is an awkward potion, and in order to make that, you need to have nether warts.

Doug finds a room in the fortress where nether warts grow. He learned that they only grow on soul sand, a special sand that will slow anyone down and slowly consume them. To make an awkward potion you need to put the nether warts on the top and up to three water-filled glass bottles on the bottom. Doug does exactly what the brewing book says, but nothing happens.

Then, Doug realizes that he must fuel the brewing stand for it to make a potion. He flips the book back a couple of pages. It says that you must grind a blaze rod to make blaze powder, which can fuel the brewing stand. So, Doug does this simply by putting it into his starter inventory.

Once the blaze rod is ground, it drops three pieces of blaze powder. Then, Doug uses the blaze powder to fuel the brewing stand. Suddenly, the brewing stand starts to release smoke. After about twenty seconds, Doug takes the potions out of the stands.

"Success!" Doug exclaims.

The next step to making a fire resistance potion is to combine the awkward potion with some magma cream. The only way to get magma cream is to get it from a magma cube. Doug walks from the bastion to see if he can see a magma cube. In the distance, Doug sees a particularly friendly magma cube. Doug walks closer.

"Hello," Doug says happily.

"Hello," the magma cube says.

"I'm going to name you 'Amber,'" Doug says.

"Yay, I like that name!" Amber exclaims.

"I wonder if I could borrow some magma

cream?" Doug asks.

"OK," Amber says. "My inventory is completely filled with magma cream. Take as much as you like."

Doug takes ten magma cream from Amber's pile of magma cream. Then, he walks to his brewing stand. This time Doug puts the magma on the top and puts the awkward potions on the bottom. The brewing stand starts to smoke again. This process is harder than making an awkward potion. After about twenty seconds, the potions are done! Doug pulls the potions out of the stands.

"It worked!" Doug exclaims.

CHAPTER 9

NETHER TREASURE

D oug walks into the bastion remnant with Cyan. Suddenly, Doug hears a slight *whoosh*. Doug looks on the right side of the bastion. There is a pig-like figure with a crossbow. It fires the crossbow at Doug, but luckily, Doug dodges the arrow.

Another pig-like figure comes from behind Doug and hits him with his gold sword. Doug realizes now that he's trapped in this bastion remnant.

More of the pig-like creatures come out of the hidden cracks that Doug did not see before. He quickly runs up one of the blackstone staircases and tries to hide on the balcony with Cyan. But the pig-like figures are smarter than he thinks. They run up the staircase and try to attack Doug, but Cyan has a plan!

Cyan asks Doug to get away from him. Once Doug is a safe distance away from him, he explodes, making a huge hole in the blackstone balcony that the pig-like figures cannot cross. Doug opens up one of the chests, making the pig-like figures extra angry with them. Doug calls the pig-like figures "piglins."

From one of the doorways that Doug did not see, a piglin with a gold sword comes out, trying to knock him off the balcony. Doug grabs the piglin and throws him off the balcony into the lava.

"Should have put a balcony rail there," Doug laughs.

The piglins start shooting arrows at Doug! Cyan jumps over the giant hole and explodes on the piglins with an even larger explosion than before.

Doug looks in the center of the cube and sees that there's a treasure room. A skeleton walks around the corner unexpectedly and shoots Doug with his bow. Luckily, Doug doesn't fall off the balcony. More skeletons start appearing from doorways, and some withered skeletons also start appearing. Even Cyan's explosion can't destroy all of the skeletons.

Cyan grabs one of his charged TNTs out of his pack. He throws it straight at the angry gang of skeletons. The TNT blows most of the skeletons into the lava, but three remain, still angry at Doug and Cyan.

Doug runs straight toward one of the skeletons and breaks off its arm. He uses the arm like a bat and hits the skeleton into the lava. Doug runs to the next skeleton and sticks his leg out to trip the skeleton. He grabs the skeleton by its spine and throws it into another skeleton, and they're both knocked into the lava.

A withered skeleton from a crack that Doug did not notice until now walks up and hits him. Doug almost falls into the lava. Luckily, he knocks the withered skeleton back into the wall. "Go back where you came from!" Doug yells. Doug grabs the withered skeleton's weak stone sword and throws it into the lava.

Cyan takes his extra explosive TNT out of his pack and throws it behind the withered skeleton. The withered skeleton is blown straight into another wall and explodes into a million pieces. There are no more skeletons to attack!

Doug walks down the staircase and goes to the treasure room. The path to the treasure room seems to be broken, so Doug and Cyan jump on a few pieces of blackstone held up by lava to get there. This is how the piglins are able to communicate through colonies of different bastions.

There are also a few blocks of glowstone and glowstone dust in the chest. Doug grabs out a few pieces of his crying obsidian and tries to make something out of these materials. He has six blocks of crying obsidian and three blocks of glowstone. Doug takes a crafting table out of his pack and starts crafting. He puts the three unique pieces of crying obsidian on top of the crafting table. He also puts three pieces of crying obsidian on the bottom of the table. Nothing happens. He figures that he needs to power it, so he pushes three glowstones into the middle of the table. Instantly, the glowstone and crying obsidian merge into one block.

There is a black disk on each side of the unique block, and the top is similar to a cauldron. Doug has five pieces of glowstone dust. He drops one of the pieces into the top of the mysterious block. Suddenly, a quarter of each of the black disks fills with a bright yellow light.

"Wow!" Doug says. He drops another piece of glowstone dust into the block. Now half of the black disks are filled with yellow light. Doug keeps dropping pieces of glowstone dust into the block, and pretty soon there are no more black disks left; there are now only yellow disks.

Doug looks from one of the cracks. There is a piglin quietly aiming his bow at Doug. He shoots Doug, knocking him into the lava.

"Nooooooooo!!!" Cyan yells.

CHAPTER 10

TAMING A HOGLIN

"**D**oug, are you OK?" Cyan yells. Cyan realizes that his friend is not lost. He looks at the respawn anchor. Suddenly, the anchor's top glows purple. Doug seems to respawn on the anchor.

"Yay! You're alive!" Cyan exclaims, "Now I'm going to try to jump into the lava!"

Doug says, "Cyan! Don't do it! The respawn anchor doesn't work for creepers, only for humans like me!"

But it's too late! Cyan has already slipped into the lava. Doug reaches into his pouch and pulls out a splash potion of fire resistance. Doug gets closer to the lava and splashes it on Cyan.

The fire resistance starts to do its work and stops Cyan from burning in the lava. Cyan climbs out of the lava, safe and sound.

"Thank you for saving me!" Cyan exclaims to Doug.

Doug replies, "I think we should try to get back to the portal, even though it's a long way back."

They walk outside to get the axolotls.

"I think we're ready to go, too," Geode and Blurple say.

Geode says, "We had fun playing with Grump-Grump while you were inside."

"We need fast transportation in order to get back to the portal," Doug says as he grabs out his map to show Geode and Blurple the way back.

"What?!" Doug exclaims, "I know that when we left the portal, I made a map to help us get back, but now the map has disappeared! Traveling across lava is too slow. We need to have a faster way in order to get there quickly. I think we should go around the lava and then seek out the portal that we came through.

"There is a lot of foliage on the left side of the lava, but there is even more foliage on the right side. I guess we should take the left side because it's easier than trekking through the right side. But I think Grump-Grump wants to go back to the portal his own way."

As they leave Grump-Grump to waddle through the lava on his way to the portal, they head into the foliage on the left side of the lava.

Suddenly, Doug and the axolotls hear a loud snort. They look behind one of the crimson trees, and there is an over-sized pig on the other side. It seems to have a tusk on each side of its head.

"This doesn't look good!" Doug exclaims. "What happened to the pig? It has black spikes on its back!"

Doug takes out one of his crimson fungi and tries to tame the hoglin with it, but the hoglin doesn't accept it. Doug tries to get a little closer to see if the hoglin will see the fungus now.

The hoglin looks at Doug and walks a little closer. Suddenly, the hoglin brings his tusks up and plows Doug into a tree.

"Oh, no!" Doug exclaims, "Why can't I move my body?"

Then Doug realizes that his head is stuck in the tree. He tries to get himself down to the ground, but he can't. The hoglin keeps using his tusks to push Doug higher and higher into the tree.

The hoglin starts to rip off Doug's pouch.

"No! Nooo!" Doug says, "Not my beautifully sewn pouch that I made myself!"

Before his pouch is ripped off, Doug grabs a crimson fungus and throws it into the hoglin's mouth. The hoglin immediately stops attacking Doug and sits on the ground.

Doug climbs down the tree and almost breaks his leg. Then he puts a saddle on the hoglin. "I'm going to name you 'Pork Chop,'" Doug says.

Doug and the rest of his friends get onto Pork Chop and head toward the portal. As the hoglin starts to walk, Doug notices that they're in an entirely new biome. It's all blue and has lots of foliage, such as new vines and new trees.

"I'm going to name this biome a 'Blue Raspberry' biome," Doug says.

Suddenly, Pork Chop trips on a branch and is catapulted into the lava. Luckily, Doug and the axolotls are able to grab onto a red vine and safely get back to the biome, avoiding the lava.

CHAPTER 11

DISCOVERING RUINS

"**P**ORK CHOP!" Doug cries. He investigates the lava but doesn't see anything.

"Nooooo!" Doug says. He grabs the stick that Pork Chop had tripped on and throws it into the lava. "There! Now no one else can trip on it!"

Doug walks around the blue raspberry biome and collects some of the foliage off one of the trees. He also collects some netherrack, grass, and warped fungus to take back to the Overworld. He's never seen these in the Overworld or in any of the other biomes that he's come across so far.

"Hmm," Doug says, "The netherrack feels like mycelium, but there is blue stuff on top of it. I'm going to name it 'warped nylium.'"

"There seem to be red and blue sprouts growing all over this biome. I'll name the red plants 'crimson roots' and the blue sprouts 'nether sprouts.' The vines seem to be growing upward and not hanging onto the trees."

Doug takes off a piece of the vines and puts it into his pack.

"I'm going to name these vines 'twisting vines.'"

"Can we climb the vines and see where they lead?" Cyan asks.

"I'll try," Doug replies.

Doug puts his hand on the vine and starts to climb it.

"The vine doesn't seem to break when I climb it. It must be strong enough to hold me."

Doug grabs Cyan and the axolotls and pulls them up with him. Doug keeps climbing with Cyan and the axolotls on his back. Suddenly, he puts his foot onto a branch of the vine, and his foot slips, making him almost fall off. But he manages to hold on.

After countless hours of climbing, Doug and his friends finally reach the top.

"We did it!" Geode cries.

"We finally reached the top!" Cyan exclaims.

Doug turns around to see a massive blackstone building, preserved because nothing has been able to climb up the vines until now.

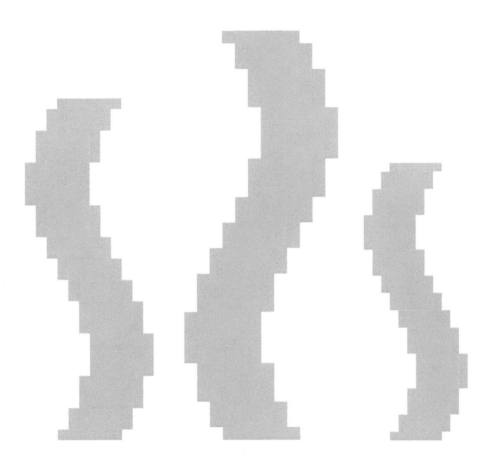

CHAPTER 12

BACK INTO THE OVERWORLD

"From this view, we should be able to see the portal," Blurple says. And just as Blurple speaks, Doug looks over the ledge to see a beautiful nether portal, the only thing that can lead them out of the Nether. It glows like the respawn anchor that Doug had created. Its obsidian is the finest he could ever imagine.

"How do we get down?" Geode asks.

"Just wait," Doug replies.

After ten minutes of waiting, Geode and Blurple are starting to get bored. Then suddenly, it happens! Cyan looks down to see that Grump-Grump is right below them, striding on the lava toward the portal.

"Now I see what you meant by waiting," Blurple

grumbles.

"Well, at least it worked," Geode says.

"If we can jump onto Grump-Grump at the right moment, then I think we can get to the portal faster," Doug explains.

After a few seconds, Doug exclaims, "Now!" He grabs the axolotls as fast as he can and jumps onto the strider. For a second, Grump-Grump does not even know that they landed on him, and he can't hold all their weight but quickly adjusts. Then Doug puts the axolotls in their leather bucket holders on each side of Grump-Grump and puts Cyan behind him. Now they're ready to get to the portal.

"Grump-Grump?" Doug asks.

"Yes?" Grump-Grump replies.

"Are you going as fast as you can?"

"Pretty much," Grump-Grump says, out of breath.

"Do you want some warped fungus on a stick?"

"Oh, yes, please!" Grump-Grump exclaims.

Doug reaches into his pack and pulls out some warped fungus, sticking to a fishing rod. Doug dangles the warped fungus right in front of Grump-Grump. Suddenly, Grump-Grump seems to get super speed!

"Wow!" Doug says, "I thought you were going as fast as you could!"

"I like to move faster when food is on the line," Grump-Grump replies.

"Now he's going much faster," Geode laughs.

Pretty soon, they reach the dock that Doug created out of crimson wood. Surprisingly, it had not burned in the lava. Now they were a few blocks away from the portal.

"We made it!" Blurple said.

The axolotls are ready to go back home and take a long rest, out of their buckets and in their lush cave. Just as they're about to walk through the portal, a fireball comes and hits the portal, making the only way home disappear!

"You psychopath!" Doug yells at the ghast. "Why did you just block our only way back to the Overworld?"

"Because I'm a ghost! Because I can shoot fireballs at anything I want! I'm the only creature that can shoot fireballs!"

"Are you?" Geode asks. "Doug can shoot fireballs!"

"It doesn't seem like he can," the ghast replies. "If he does have fireballs, he would be launching them at me right now."

And with that being said, the ghast launches a fireball at Doug.

Suddenly, Doug grabs out his netherite sword and hits the fireball with as much power as he can. The fireball deflects off the sword and is launched toward the ghast.

"The tables are turned!" Doug exclaims.

"Wait! What? Noooooo," the ghast cries, and he explodes into a million pieces. All that is left is a ghast tear which Doug picks up and puts into his pack. The ghast tear is as hard as a rock.

Luckily, Doug has an extra flint and steel and re-lights the portal. Geode, Blurple, Doug, and Cyan all jump into the portal at the same time.

When they come back out of the portal, they're not in the Nether anymore, they're in their own lush caves.

"I love it!" Cyan says as he enjoys the beautiful, lush caves.

"I have a special surprise for you, Geode and Blurple!" Cyan exclaims.

He has a glass box strapped on his back, but it seems that there is nothing inside of it until Cyan opens it in the lush caves. Suddenly, a powder-blue axolotl climbs out of the box. It somehow had been invisible to the rest of the axolotls and Doug until now.

"Wait! Is that Snowy?" Geode and Blurple ask.

"Hello!" Snowy exclaims. "I drank a potion of invisibility. That way I could surprise you. I like your lush cave!" Snowy says as he waddles into the water with the axolotls, and they start to have a water fight.

They lived happily ever after, with more adventures to come!

FACT FILE

- This special type of salamander lives only in the canals and rivers in regions of Mexico like Lake Xochimilco.

- Axolotls can even regrow limbs. If one of an axolotl's limbs is removed, it'll regrow the limb in a short amount of time, specifically, in 40 to 50 days.

- You may have recognized what an axolotl looks like. Its body is milky pink, and its gills are slightly darker, but wild axolotls are usually a shade of brown colored to match the mud of the rivers in Mexico. The axolotl has many variants of colors including golden, albino, pink, and a wild variant.

- Axolotls often seem to have emotions on their faces. Mostly you can see his or her little smiley face smiling back at you.

- Axolotls may seem cute, but they're actually predators. They eat small fish, tadpoles, other salamanders, and small crustaceans.

- Also, you may notice and wonder where the gills on the axolotls' heads are. Strangely, the gills of the axolotl are the feathery limbs coming from the sides of their heads.

- The main reason axolotls are endangered is that big fish that live in the same rivers and ponds that axolotls thrive in eat the axolotls' small eggs. There are other reasons too, such as pollution and the size of their home decreasing from human population expansion.

- The axolotl was chosen as the first official national emoji for Mexico City and is also the first city to launch an official emoji.

See you in our next adventure in book 4,
The Axolotl:
Beating the Ender Dragon

Doug, Geode, Blurple, and Snowy

CPSIA information can be obtained
at www.ICGtesting.com
Printed in the USA
BVHW090607221221
624594BV00019B/1850